MARGRET & H.A. REY'S

Curious George in THE BIG SURPRISE!

Hats Off!

It's your birthday

Houghton Mifflin Harcourt

Boston   New York

hmhco.com

Written by Liza Charlesworth
Illustrations by Artful Doodlers Ltd.

The text was set in Adobe Garamond Pro.
The display type was set in Marvin Regular.

ISBN 978-1-328-87443-6

Manufactured in China
SCP 10 9 8 7 6 5 4 3 2
4500746619

No, that is
not right.

Later that day . . .
You want me to read the WHOLE thing?!
Oh, my!
Happy Birthday

Get your child ready to read in three simple steps!

1 **I READ**	Read the book to your child.
 **2** **WE READ**	Read the book together.
 **3** **YOU READ**	Encourage your child to read the book over and over again.

31901064288592